The Sender Feels Better

series has been created to sow

seeds in children's hearts,

helping them find different

ways of coping with new

situations

Sender is a jolly soul

He jumps and spins and skips

But on Wednesday, he went too fast

And into a tree he flips

Sender bumps his hand into the trunk

And crumples to the mud

His arms and legs land in a heap

His body with a thud

Sender feels a tear well in his eye

First right then left eye too

His hand starts to go all **red**

He doesn't know what to do

Sender's friend Goo was fast to soothe

He checks that he's ok

"I'll make sure that you're alright"

Goo knows just what to say

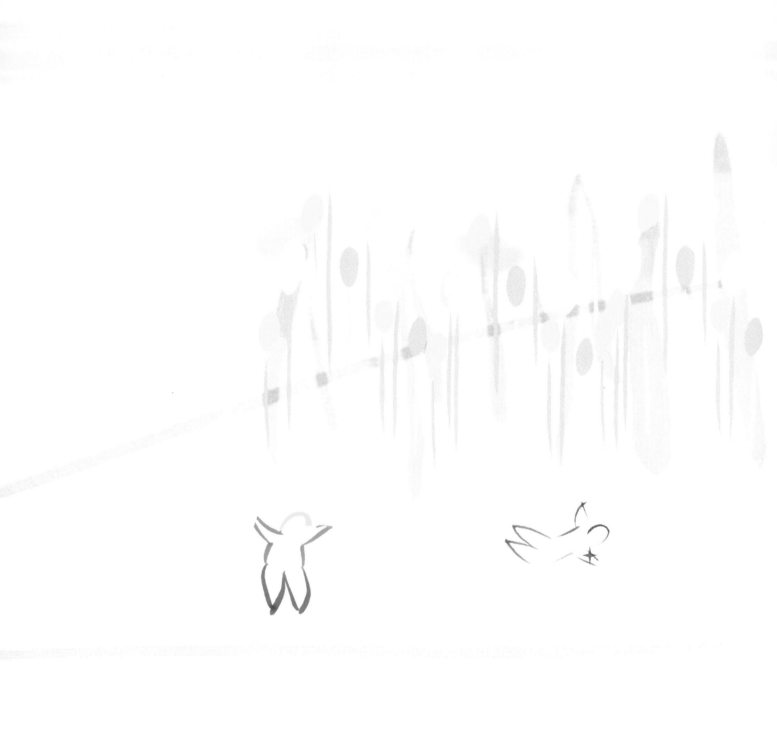

Sender's shock makes him feel weary

He doesn't make a sound

So Eny rushes to help Goo out
They lift Sender off the ground

Sender's arms lock with his pals

They walk him to his home

His hand feels sore but he gives a smile

He is **glad** not to be alone

Sender's shock is wearing off now

And he is feeling much more calm

But his hand is red and really sore

The pain travelling up his arm

Sender's pal Eny says what to do

He needs to rest some more

Because when you sleep your soldiers wake

And fix where it's all sore

Sender's soldiers live within his body

And sleep throughout the days

They save their **energy** for every night

Working when sleeping Sender lays

Sender knows he needs more sleep

His hand needs lots of patching

It's sore right now so off he nods

To start his army marching

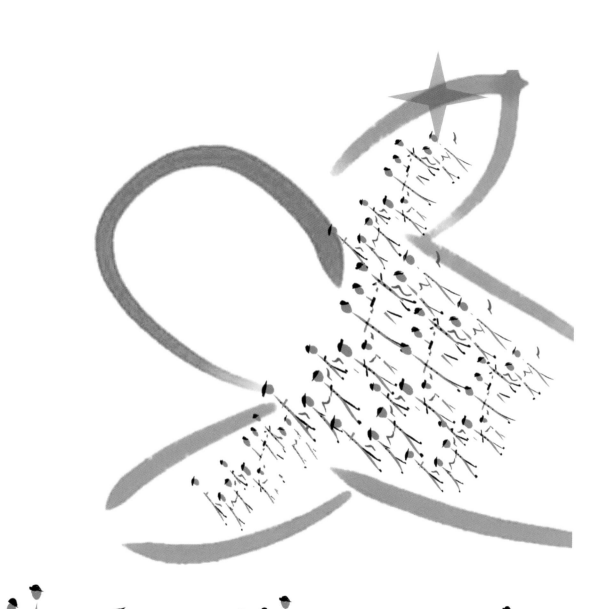

Sender's soldiers move to his sore hand

But only when he's sound a-snooze

They work all night to mend his pain

For this there is no time to lose

Sender wakes up when the sun streams in
Thursday morning has begun

He can tell though almost straight away
His soldiers' work is not quite done

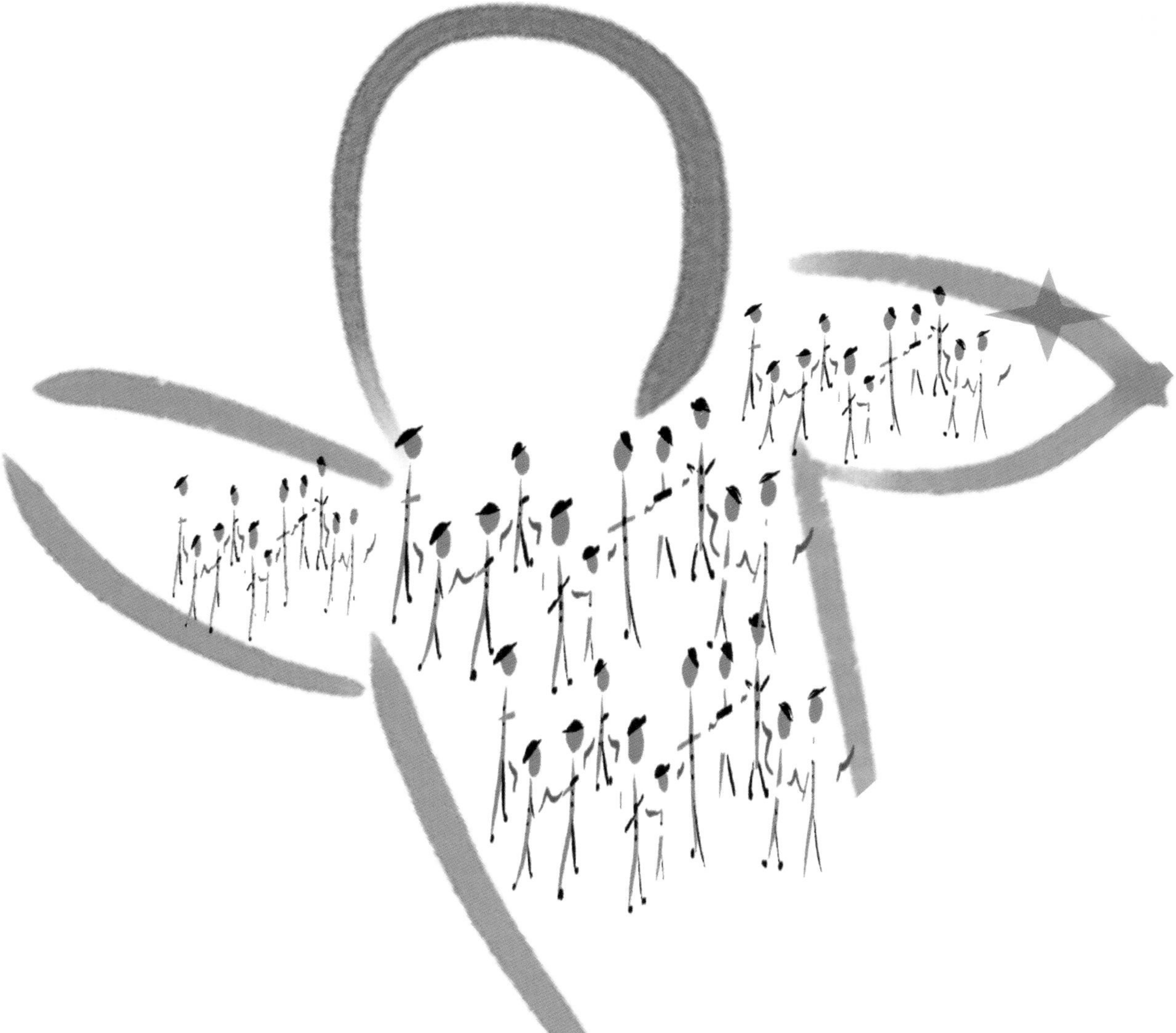

Sender's soldiers need more than one full night

His hand took quite a **knock**

Sometimes they need to fix the pain

And also fix the shock

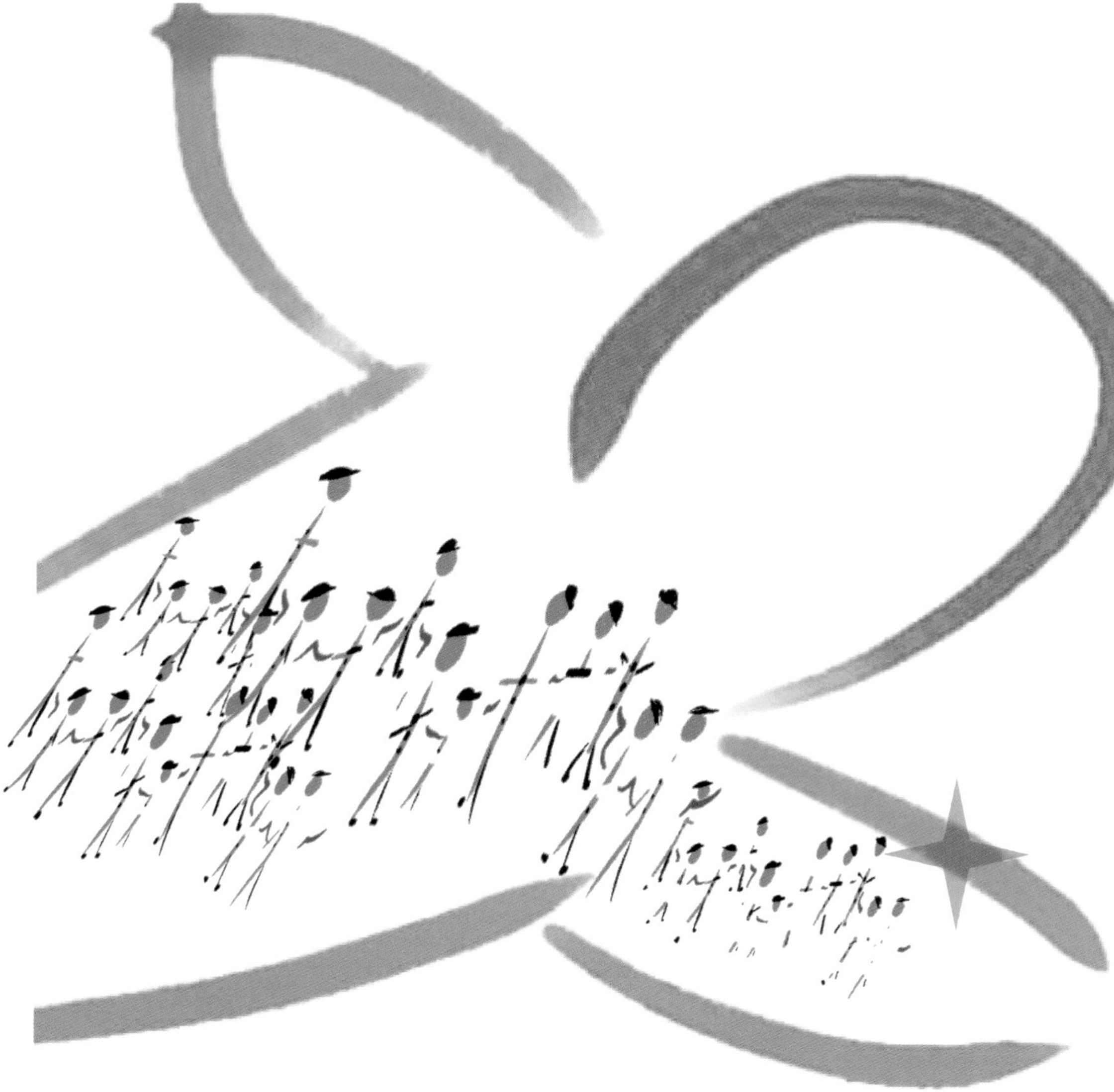

Sender needs another good sleep

So an early night he gets

His hand feels better but not tip- top

His soldiers will do their best

Sender sleeps till Friday dawn

And jumps out of bed with cheer

He has no more pain in his poor hand

Although the redness is still there

Sender's red may fade or it may stay

Beyond this week or for many years

But as long as he can play pain free

It matters not how his hand appears

Sender calls his friends to come outside

He can't wait to meet, laugh and sing

It still looks sore but he feels no pain

His soldiers are a-maz-ing

For Sebastian

Because your joy is infectious

And even your little soldiers work overtime for you

Have you read Sender Chooses Fun?

Look out for more books in the Sender series!

Printed in Great Britain
by Amazon